and **stare** . . .

and . . .

stare.

Every day, Bear emerged from his cave and **stared** at the first thing he saw.

One morning, he **stared** at a family of ladybirds who were having their breakfast on a small leaf.

"What are you **staring** at?" squeaked the daddy ladybird. "We're trying to have our breakfast in peace!"

And with that, they scuttled off to find somewhere else to eat.

Bear strolled further into the forest
and climbed a big tree.

He **stared** at a bird feeding
her chicks in their nest.

"Can I help you?" asked the bird.
Bear did not answer. He just **stared.**

The chicks did not like Bear **staring** at them.

He was putting them off their dinner.

"Go on, sshhhooooo!" squawked the bird.

"Get down on the ground where you belong!"

Bear climbed back down to the forest floor where he spied a badger's sett.

He poked his head into the entrance . . . and I'm sure you can guess what happened next.

"Oi! Stop **gawking!**" barked the badger,
and he bit poor Bear on his nose.

(He was a particularly angry badger.)

Bear pulled his head from the badger's sett with a
**POP!**

and skulked off, rubbing his sore nose.

Before long, Bear found a log to sit on
by a large, green pond.

He sat and pondered by the pond.

Bear didn't mean to annoy all the other animals. He was just naturally curious but too shy to say anything.

"I've seen that look before," said a small, croaky voice coming from the pond.

Bear looked down and saw a plump little frog. Bear **stared** at the frog.

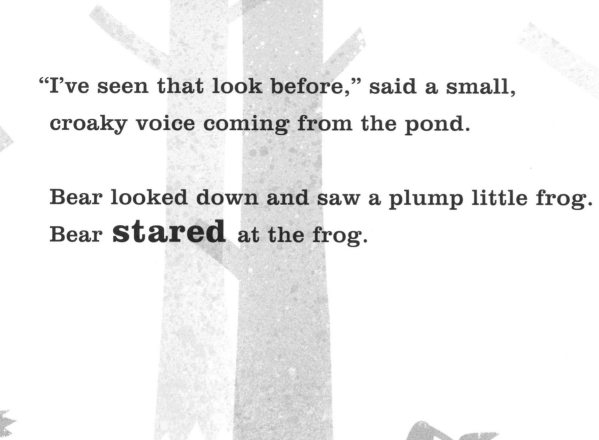

The frog **stared** back with his big, goggly eyes.

"Not much fun being **stared** at, is it?"
continued the frog.

"I suppose not," muttered Bear. "It's just that I don't
know what to say to anyone, and before I've had a
chance to think, it's too late."

Bear **stared** into the water . . .
and saw another bear **staring** back at him
with the same wide, curious eyes.
He looked just like Bear in every way, but this bear
wobbled and was a strange green colour.

Then something extraordinary happened.
The green bear blinked, and his mouth
turned into a **smile** . . .

. . . which turned into a big, **happy** grin.

"You see?" said the frog. "Sometimes a **smile** is all you need. I may have big, goggly, **starey** eyes, but I also have the widest smile in the whole forest."

Then the frog showed Bear his biggest, widest, happiest **smile**, before diving off into the water.

As the frog disappeared,
so too did the wobbly, green bear.

The next day, Bear trudged out of his cave.
He saw the ladybird family enjoying their
breakfast on a small leaf.

The daddy ladybird was just about to gather
up their things and leave, when Bear said,
"Hello!" with a big **smile** on his face.

"Oh, hello!" replied the daddy ladybird,
and he **smiled** back.

Bear strolled happily off into the forest.

Bear made lots of new friends that day,
and did not feel the need to **stare.**

Although . . .

. . . he did have one new friend who didn't mind Bear **staring** at him . . .

And he was just as good at **staring** back.

For Avarin (our bear cub).

**A TEMPLAR BOOK**

First published in the UK in 2015 by Templar Publishing,
Part of the Bonnier Publishing Group
The Plaza, 535 King's Road, London, SW10 0SZ
www.templarco.co.uk
www.bonnierpublishing.com

ISBN 978-1-78370-374-6 Hardback
ISBN 978-1-78370-375-3 Paperback

Edited by Alison Ritchie
Designed by Genevieve Webster

Printed in China

**t**

**templar** publishing